ANIMAL VS. ANIMAL

WHO'S THE
BENDIEST?

BY EMILIE DUFRESNE

Please visit our website, www.garethstevens.com. For a free color catalog of all our high-quality books, call toll free 1-800-542-2595 or fax 1-877-542-2596.

Library of Congress Cataloging-in-Publication Data
Names: Dufresne, Emilie.
Title: Who's the bendiest? / Emilie Dufresne.
Description: New York : Gareth Stevens Publishing, 2022. | Series: Animal vs. animal | Includes glossary and index.
Identifiers: ISBN 9781534537309 (pbk.) | ISBN 9781534537323 (library bound) | ISBN 9781534537316 (6 pack) | ISBN 9781534537330 (ebook)
Subjects: LCSH: Morphology (Animals)--Juvenile literature. | Animals--Juvenile literature.
Classification: LCC QL799.3 D843 2022 | DDC 591.4'1--dc23

Published in 2022 by
Gareth Stevens Publishing
29 East 21st Street
New York, NY 10010

© 2022 Booklife Publishing
This edition is published by arrangement with Booklife Publishing

Edited by: Holly Duhig
Designed by: Danielle Rippengill

All rights reserved. No part of this book may be reproduced in any form without permission in writing from the publisher, except by a reviewer.

Printed in the United States of America

Some of the images in this book illustrate individuals who are models. The depictions do not imply actual situations or events.

CPSIA compliance information: Batch #CSGS22: For further information contact Gareth Stevens, New York, New York at 1-800-542-2595.

Find us on

IMAGE CREDITS

All images are courtesy of Shutterstock.com, unless otherwise specified. With thanks to Getty Images, Thinkstock Photo, and iStockphoto. Cover – Ovocheva, Stepova Oksana, Abscent. Images used on every page – Ovocheva, Stepova Oksana. 5 – ONYXprj, Abscent. 6&7 – Guingm. 8 – EB Adventure Photography. 9 – Stan Shebs [GFDL (http://www.gnu.org/copyleft/fdl.html), CC BY-SA 3.0 (https://creativecommons.org/licenses/by-sa/3.0) or CC BY-SA 2.5 (https://creativecommons.org/licenses/by-sa/2.5)], from Wikimedia Commons. 8&9 – Guingm. 10&11 – Abscent. 12 – otsphoto. 13 – turtix. 12&13 – Guingm. 14&15 – ArchOnez, Abscent. 16 – Vladimir Wrangel. 17 – Irina Kozorog. 16&17 – Guingm. 18&19 – Abscent. 20&21 – amiloslava. 22 – Guingm. 23 – Abscent.

CONTENTS

- **PAGE 4** — The Great and Small Games
- **PAGE 6** — The Contenders
- **PAGE 8** — Sea Lion vs. Hagfish
- **PAGE 10** — The Knot Tie
- **PAGE 12** — Ferret vs. Cat
- **PAGE 14** — The Tunnel Turn
- **PAGE 16** — Octopus vs. Rat
- **PAGE 18** — The Squish-a-Thon
- **PAGE 20** — Hall of Fame
- **PAGE 22** — Quiz and Activity
- **PAGE 24** — Glossary and Index

Words that look like this can be found in the glossary on page 24.

THE GREAT AND SMALL GAMES

Step right up!
It's the Great and Small Games!
See nature's bendiest and most flexible creatures in action!

Today's events:
The Knot Tie!
The Tunnel Turn!
The Squish-a-Thon!

These events will surely decide once and for all:
Who's the Bendiest?

THE CONTENDERS

Let's find out some facts and figures about today's contenders!

Rat
The Big Squeeze

Size: 5 inches (12.7 cm) long

Lives: Worldwide

Stretch Stats: Wriggling through holes the size of its head

Cat
The Flexi-Feline

Size: 18 inches (45.7 cm) long

Lives: Worldwide

Stretch Stats: Can rotate its body in two different directions while in the air

Ferret
The Rotating Rodent

Size: 24 inches (61 cm) long, including tail

Lives: Europe, Asia, Africa, and North America

Stretch Stats: Super stretchy spine

Octopus
The Boneless Blob

Size: Around 3 feet (1 m) long

Lives: Tropical and **temperate** oceans

Stretch Stats: Can squeeze through tiny gaps

Hagfish
Slip 'n' Slide

Size: Over 3 feet (1 m) long

Lives: Cold waters across the world

Stretch Stats: Can twist and turn into different shapes

Californian Sea Lion
Roly Poly Pup

Size: Up to 8 feet (2.4 m) long

Lives: North America

Stretch Stats: Very flexible neck

SEA LION VS.

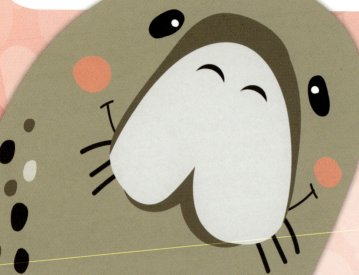

Rrrrrround Onnnne!

ARP! ARP!

This sea lion is super stretchy and bendy. With a head that can be bent all the way back so that he can look behind him, you would think this animal didn't have a neck!

Nickname:
Roly Poly Pup

Flexi-Fact: Being able to bend their necks all the way back means that sea lions can make sharp turns in the water.

HAGFISH

This bendy bottom-feeder lives in the depths of the ocean and feeds on rotting **carcasses**. But he always makes time to stretch, and is one of the most flexible animals in the world.

Nickname:
Slip 'n' Slide

Flexi-Fact: With a skull but no spine, hagfish can twist and turn into all sorts of shapes!

Hagfish have very loose skin that helps them to bend into any shape without tearing.

LET'S TWIST

THE KNOT TIE

Contenders, to test your flexibility we will be doing the knot tie! Whoever can tie themselves into a knot first will be the winner. The sea lion is trying his best to twist his body around, but bending his neck is the best he can do.

Sea lions also have very flexible hips that let them move on land very easily by <u>rotating</u> their flippers under their body.

FERRET VS.

Rrrrrrround Twoooo!

DOOK! DOOK!

This wriggly weasel can worm his way through any gap. Ferrets have very long spines that help them turn in tight spaces.

Nickname: The Rotating Rodent

Flexi-Fact: Humans have 33 **vertebrae** (say: ver-tuh-bray) in their spine, while ferrets have 46. That's a lot more places to bend!

CAT

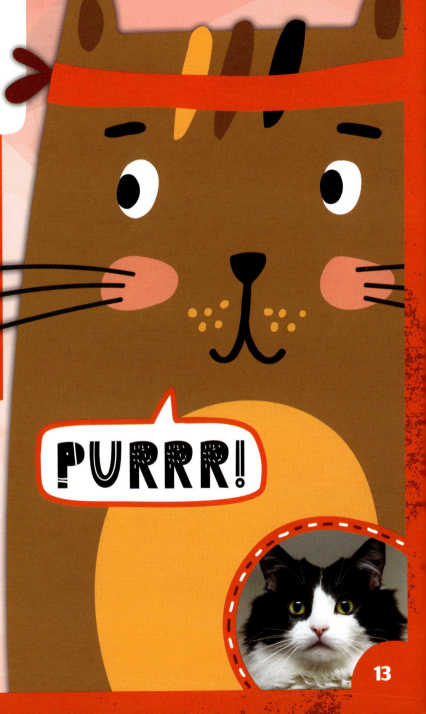

Our feline friend has a fiercely flexible trick up his sleeve. If he falls from high up, he can rotate his body really quickly and always land on his feet!

Nickname: The Flexi-Feline

Flexi-Fact: A cat uses its whiskers to know whether it can fit into a space or not!

Cats have flexible spines; this helps them perform amazing tricks, such as jumping nine times their height!

PURRR!

THE TUNNEL TURN

Each contender has a tunnel not much wider than they are. They must enter the tunnel, turn around, and come back out. The first animal out of the tunnel is the winner!

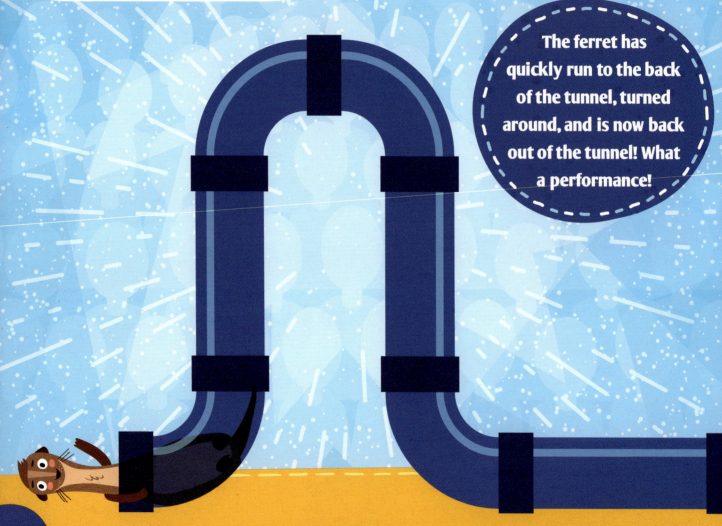

The ferret has quickly run to the back of the tunnel, turned around, and is now back out of the tunnel! What a performance!

OCTOPUS

Rrrrrrround Threee!

With amazing **camouflage** and the ability to ward off predators with a squirt of ink, the Boneless Blob is ready to squeeze himself into first place.

Nickname:
The Boneless Blob

Flexi-Fact:
Octopuses can squeeze their **bulbous** heads through any gap that their beaks can fit through.

VS. RAT

A mischievous yet **malleable** creature, this contender is ready for the big squeeze! With razor-sharp teeth that can chew through metal, this rat is not messing around.

Nickname:
The Big Squeeze

Flexi-Fact:
Rats have folding rib cages that help them squeeze through holes as small as 1 inch (2.5 cm) wide!

The outer layer of a rat's tooth is harder than platinum.

NIBBLE! NIBBLE!

THE SQUISH-A-THON

Both contenders will have to twist and bend their bodies into weird and wonderful positions to try to get out of the tiny hole they are faced with.

When moving through a small gap, an octopus will move legs first and pull his head out last.

HALL OF FAME

Great Horned Owl
This creature can turn its head up to 270 degrees.

Lives: North and South America

Eats: Small animals such as mice

Size: 25 inches (63.5 cm) tall, 5-foot (1.5 m) wingspan

Worm
Having no skeleton lets this worm wriggle his way through life.

Lives: Europe, North America, and western Asia

Eats: Soil, leaves, and poop

Size: Up to 14 inches (35.6) cm long

Elephant
Elephant trunks are very flexible and have strong muscles.

Lives: South Asia, Southeast Asia, and sub-Saharan Africa

Eats: Trees, leaves, and plants

Size: Over 10 feet (3 m) tall

Spider Monkey
These monkeys have strong, flexible tails that help them climb.

Lives: Central and South America

Eats: Nuts, fruit, eggs, and spiders

Size: 26 inches (66 cm) long

QUIZ AND...

We've seen the creatures stretch and twist, and it's now time to see who's cleverest!

Questions

1. How big must a hole be for an octopus to squeeze through it?

2. What helps sea lions make tight turns in the water?

3. What can a hagfish produce when it feels threatened?

4. How many vertebrae does a ferret have?

5. What part of its body does a cat use to know whether or not it can fit into a space?

6. What hard material can rats chew through?

... ACTIVITY

How flexible are you? Try some of these moves to see how flexible you are! Can you make funny faces? For example, can you raise one eyebrow while pulling the other one down? Now try these stretches!

Bend over forward and keep your knees straight. How close can you get your hands to the ground?

Sit on the ground with your back straight. How far apart can you stretch your legs?

Answers from page 22: 1. As big as its beak 2. Being able to bend their neck all the way back 3. Slime 4. 46 5. Its whiskers 6. Metal

GLOSSARY

bulbous big and round
camouflage traits that allow an animal to hide itself in a habitat
carcass the body of a dead animals
malleable can be made to change shape
predator an animal that eats other animals for food
prey animals that are eaten by other animals for food
rotate to turn in a circle around a fixed point
temperate describing a place that is usually a mild temperature
threatened frightened or scared of something
vertebrae the small bones that make up the spine
wingspan the distance between the tips of a bird's wings

INDEX

bodies 6, 10–11, 13, 18
boneless 7, 16
cat 6, 13, 15
ferret 6, 12, 14–15
flexible 4–5, 7, 9–10, 13, 21, 23
hagfish 7, 9, 11

knots 4, 10–11
legs 18, 23
necks 7–8, 10
octopus 7, 16, 18–19
sea lion 7–8, 10
stretch 8–9, 22–23